SUPERKITTY
VERSUS
MOUSEZILLA

For Mark, the superhero who makes anything possible - HW

For my super Dove Street Studio pals - PB

SIMON & SCHUSTER

First published in Great Britain in 2020 by Simon & Schuster UK Ltd
1st Floor, 222 Gray's Inn Road, London, WC1X 8HB • A CBS Company
Text copyright © 2020 Hannah Whitty • Illustrations copyright © 2020 Paula Bowles
The right of Hannah Whitty and Paula Bowles to be identified as the author and illustrator
of this work has been asserted by them in accordance with the Copyright, Designs and
Patents Act, 1988 • All rights reserved, including the right of reproduction in whole or
in part in any form • A CIP catalogue record for this book is available from
the British Library upon request • 978-1-4711-7512-1 (PB)
978-1-4711-7513-8 (ebook) • Printed in China
1 3 5 7 9 10 8 6 4 2

HANNAH
WHITTY

PAULA
BOWLES

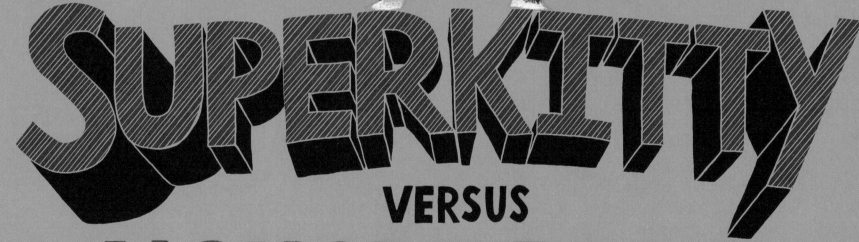

SUPERKITTY

VERSUS
MOUSEZILLA

SIMON & SCHUSTER

London   New York   Sydney   Toronto   New Delhi

It was the day of Big City's Picnic Party in the Park and I'd called all the Sensational Superheroes to the office.

"We deserve a day off!" I said to the others.
"Let's go and buy some tasty picnic treats."

First we went to the sweet shop,
but ALL the sweets had vanished!
Mr Fudge was baffled.

Then we went to Mr Fizz's pop shop,
but the bottles were all empty!

"Oh no! Someone must have drunk my last
bottle of super-special secret pop," said Mr Fizz.

"I'm sorry, Kitty. I know this is your favourite."

When we arrived at Mrs Appleton's bakery, Elephant was so excited to buy his favourite Peanut Butter Puff Cake . . .

but there were only crumbs left!

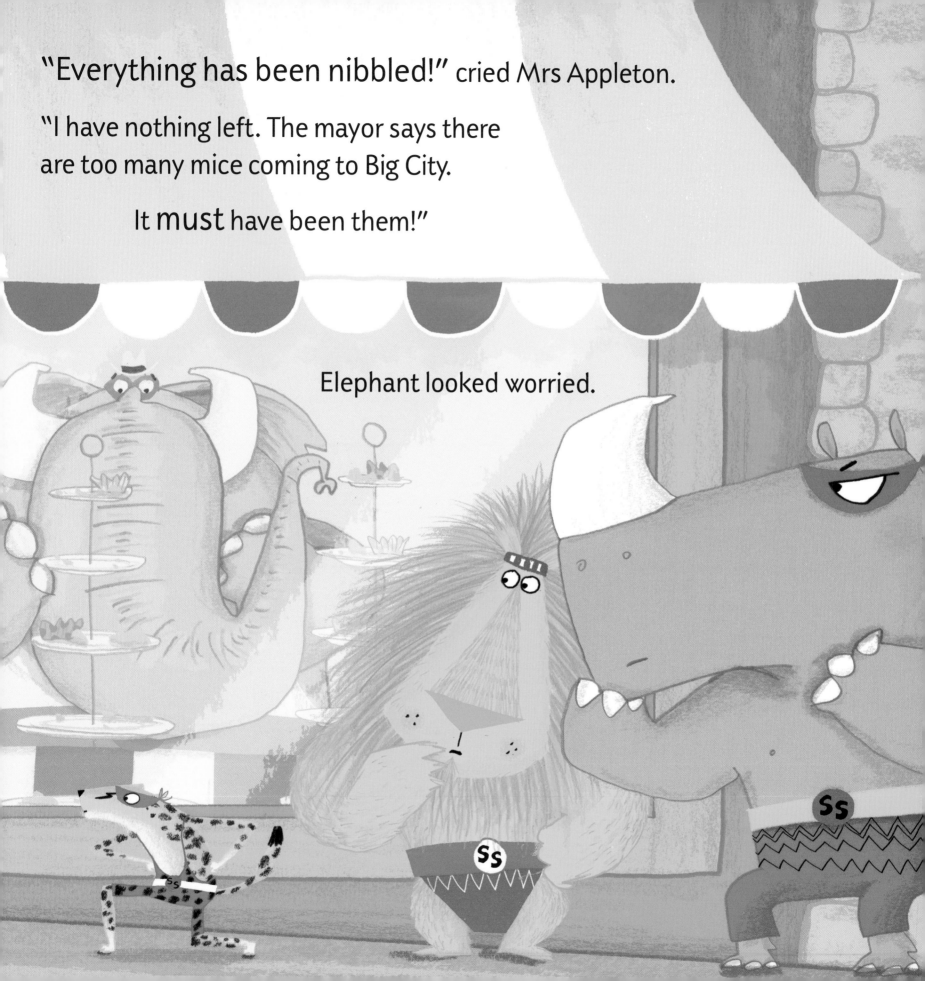

"Everything has been nibbled!" cried Mrs Appleton.

"I have nothing left. The mayor says there are too many mice coming to Big City.

It must have been them!"

Elephant looked worried.

"There's no proof that it was mice who ate the cakes," I said, "but don't worry Mrs Appleton, let us investigate. We'll get to the bottom of this!"

"We should start at the cheese shop," said Lion.
"Everyone knows that mice LOVE cheese."

When we arrived, Chef Roquefort was VERY upset.

"Sacré bleu, my cheese wheel! It's gone!" he cried.
"It must have been stolen by those terrible mice!"

VINTAGE

RETRO

1st Prize

Do not touch!

SK

SS

"Don't worry, Chef!" I cried. "We'll catch the thief!"

As we hurried through Big City looking for clues, lots of people were talking about the mice and the missing food.
"The picnic will have to be cancelled!" said Bear.

WANTED
?
$1,000,000

"What if we run out of EVERYTHING?" said Wildebeest.
"We have to find these mice and stop them!" said Rhino.

"But we don't have any proof it's the mice," I reminded them.

Suddenly, we heard the strangest noise!

BooM!
BooM!
BooM!

I froze. My whiskers were quivering.
"What was that?"

"We'd better find out!"
said Cheetah.

As we hurried after him, the sound got louder and louder.

Boom! Boom! Boom!

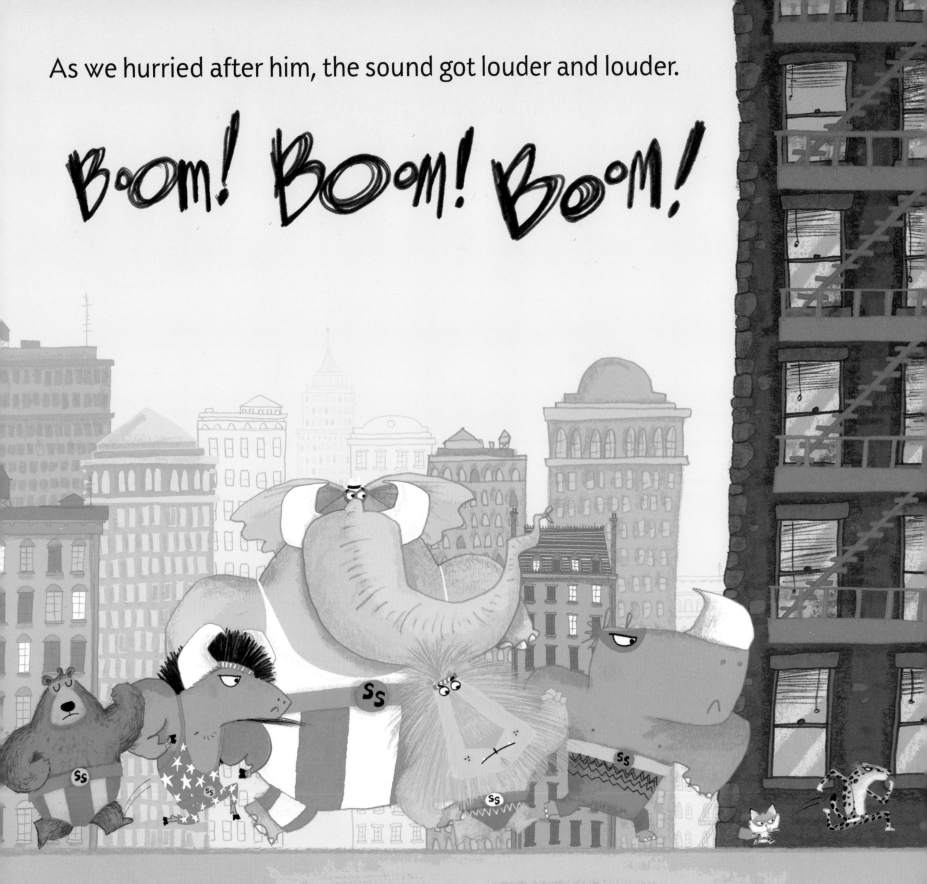

It sounded like gigantic footsteps!

The great booming noise shook Big City,
shattering windows and causing buildings to sway.

What was behind all this? Something wasn't right.
Then just as we turned the corner we saw . . .

. . . a HUGE Mousezilla. It was towering over the city
and had the mayor in one gigantic paw!

Quick as a flash we leapt into action.

But as we raced towards it, the gigantic mouse-monster started to fall apart . . . it was actually lots of little mice all working together!

"Oh, Kitty," they said, "we're so glad you're here. We need your help."

"Why should we help you? You've been stealing food from Big City!" said Elephant.
"No, no it wasn't us!" cried the mice. "It was Puss in Suits!

He's never liked mice! He took all our food and ruined our homes. Now he's pretending to be your mayor, so he can steal your food and blame us!

We had to work together to become a big mouse, so we could tell everyone and stop him. And now, look!" the mice said, as they pulled away the mayor's disguise.

I could not believe my whiskers! The mayor was, indeed, none other than the crooked cat burglar, Puss in Suits!

"I would have got away with it if it wasn't for those meddlesome mice!" he shouted.

"I'm so sorry you were blamed for the stolen food," I said to the mice. "We could use your super Mousezilla skills in the Sensational Superheroes, if you'll forgive us?"

The mice helped us rescue the real mayor from Suits Towers and he threw a new Picnic Party in the Park in their honour.

The Sensational Superheroes are super happy to have
some new superheroes on the team . . .

... even Elephant!

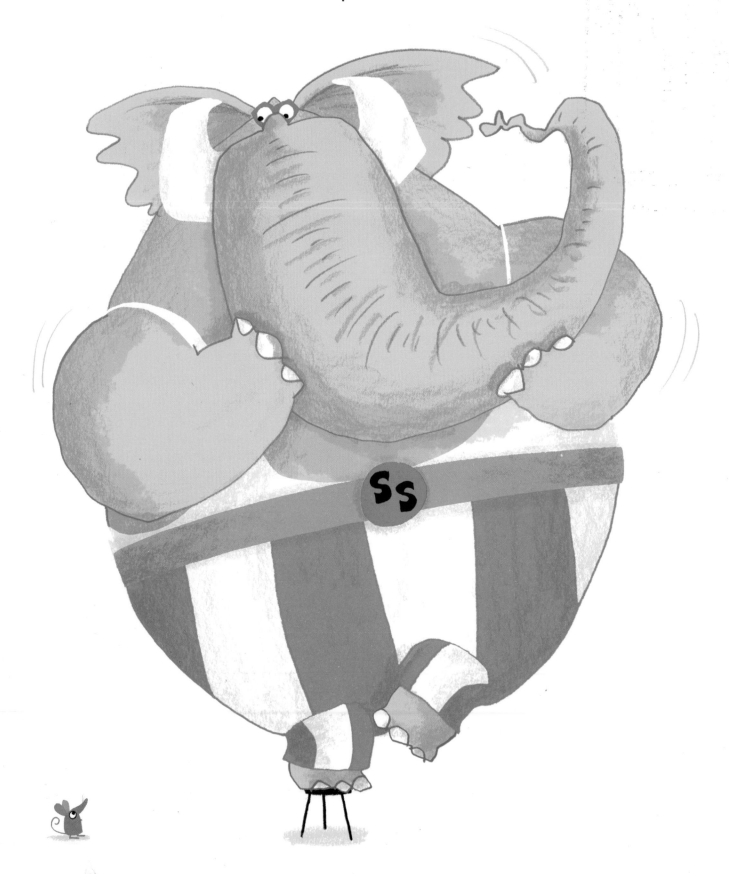